MUNICH

By

Guy Charles

Dedicated to my darling wife, who isn't Sue,
and all the Phil's I've ever worked for.

Contents

Chapter One - The job

It was a typical damp, grey, dreary English October morning as Rob made his way through the plodding traffic down the M5 towards his office on the outskirts of Bristol. It was a journey he took most weekdays, and, on most days, he would have no recollection of it when he arrived. The other cars just seeming to form a blurred mass, devoid of human life, with just anonymous, faceless beings at the helm.

Rob was, in most ways, a typical middle-aged, middle-class guy. A little paunchy but not in bad shape for his early fifties, with his own hair and teeth, most of the former being on his head which he felt was a bonus. Physically, he was unremarkable, a middle-aged guy in a suit, a corporate clone amongst millions just like him.

His life was, to all intents and purposes, successful by most standards. He had a loving wife, Sue, and three children whom he adored. Between his work income and his wife's small business, they managed to afford a comfortable but not extravagant lifestyle with a large, modern, detached house in a village on the edge of the Cotswolds.

Rob's work had, over the years, seen him work in a number of pretty tough industries from mining to oil field exploration. But, for the last 10 years, he'd been working as an environmental impact specialist for a consultancy business, mainly undertaking contracts for the government.

His background had instilled some mental toughness that many of his colleagues seemed to lack, he was a nice guy but there was an inner grit. He was seen as a good guy to have in your corner in a shitty situation and that tended to mean that's where he'd keep ending up.

So, against this background of relative stability, Rob and his family had grown and made plans for their future together, all nicely mapped out into their eventual old age and retirement. Now, Julia was approaching 18, Simon was 16 and the youngest, Kate was 15, so the fledging of Rob and Sue's chicks was looking ever closer.

But, as with so many well laid plans, the real world has a nasty habit of intervening in the most seemingly random of ways, with no prior warning. As if to demonstrate chaos theory on a personal scale, the smallest decisions or actions can have impacts on people's lives beyond all their reasonable expectation.

And so it was to be with Rob that day, although it would be much, much later before the effects came to bear and he would be consumed by the looming vortex.

Rob pulled up outside his office, a soulless 1980s concrete and glass cube farm with little to distinguish it from the other, similar corporate internment camps dotted along the bland, grey avenue on the business park.

It was one of many such buildings, the sort of places where people could toil away for years but still be unable to answer the question "what do you actually do at work, Dad"? Nobody could ever answer that question to their children when the honest answer was "wish my life away, one sorry day at a time".

Rob parked his car, strolled across the grey skied car park to the office and made his way to his desk on the first floor. Once at his desk, he fired up his laptop and wandered to the kitchen for a mug of coffee (or whatever was masquerading as coffee on that day, at the whim of the latest cost cutting initiative).

Mug in hand, he headed back to his desk pondering what exactly the steaming brown liquid might actually taste like today. On his desk, beside the laptop slowly whirring into life, he noticed a sticky note from his boss, Phil, which simply said "might have something interesting for you, Phil."

So, with his interest raised, Rob went upstairs to see Phil and find out more.

Rob was a little wary of this as, from experience, Phil's idea of "interesting" could often be alternatively described as a "shit show". But he had to at least go through the motions and humour whatever Phil's latest mad cap pet project was.

"Just the man"! Phil spouted out as Rob came into view.

"I've got something right up your street, or should I say Strasse" he grinned inanely.

What an absolute knob, thought Rob. He'd forgotten that Phil was the sort of character that nobody would query if he vanished around the time his wife had the patio extended.

"How do you fancy a spell in Germany, courtesy of HMG"?

"Well…." started Rob but Phil cut over him.

"It'll be great, all lager and bratwurst, mate."

You're an absolute arsehole, thought Rob, but decided a more diplomatic approach would be appropriate.

"So, what's the deal then, Phil"? he asked.

"It's an awesome job, mate. They're setting up a European hub office for environmental protection and HMG want one of our specialists to be involved, so that's you, matey."

"OK" said Rob hesitantly, "where, when and how long seem like obvious questions."

"At least you didn't start with how much", Phil was really starting to grate on Rob's nerves now.

"I was waiting for the answers to the other three first" replied Rob.

"Well…. it's in Munich, from next month…..for a year….to start with"

"Christ, Phil, that'll make for an interesting discussion with my wife! I'm just popping out, see you in 12 months!"

"Well, obviously you get paid trips back and we can probably do one week a month in the UK office."

"A minor issue to raise, Phil. I don't speak German, that might be a minor problem."

"Nah, they all speak really good English over there, mate, so no problem at all."

"And now the how much question" Rob asked with some trepidation in case the answer was twenty quid a week extra or some such nonsense, as often seemed to be the case.

"All travel and subsistence paid, plus 20% uplift on your salary while you're there. Sound good?"

"OK, sounds good enough to have the conversation when I get home tonight, but I can't make any promises."

"Awesome, it'll all be vorsprung durch technik, mate" quipped Phil.

Bloody hell, thought Rob, it'd be worth going to Munich just get away from this absolute arse as he walked away from Phil's desk.

Back at his desk, Rob texted his wife "interesting work stuff to talk about later. X"

The rest of the day passed with just his usual project work going on, but Rob was pondering the Munich opportunity, and whether he could make it work with their other family commitments.

At 5pm, Rob leaned back in his chair, stretched his arms over his head and then shut down his laptop. Grabbing his jacket from his chair back, Rob walked away from his desk with a cheery exclamation to his colleagues as he passed.

"Time to make like a shepherd and get the flock out of here, guys."

The drive home was a daze, Rob was so deep in thought, but he'd given the Munich opportunity plenty of brain time and knew how he would discuss it with Sue.

He waited until after the family had finished dinner and the children had dispersed to their various teenage hobbit holes to watch iPads or play on X-boxes or whatever it was they actually did in there.

As he and Sue cleared the post dinner carnage from the dining table and kitchen, he struck up the conversation.

"Sooo…I've got a new project Phil wants me to do."

"Sounds like there's a 'but' coming" said Sue suspiciously "otherwise we wouldn't be talking about it."

Sue was nobody's fool, they'd been together for almost 20 years, long enough for her to be able to see through him at a time like this.

"OK, it's twelve months with 20% more money, and sounds interesting."

"The catch"? Sue asked, "there's got to be a catch."

"I'd have to live in Germany" Rob half muttered, waiting for a verbal explosion of consternation from his wife.

It didn't come. Instead, she thought for a moment and then caught him completely off guard.

"That might not be such a crazy idea" she said "I've been meaning to tell you that my work is drying up a bit at the moment. So, the extra money would be good, and I'll be at home more for the kids, anyway"

"Oh" said Rob with some surprise "so you think I should go for it then"?

"Yes, it's got to be worth us trying, at least. I mean, what's the worst that could happen? We'll manage it somehow."

So, with those few innocuous words, Rob and Sue had unknowingly set the butterfly wings of their own personal chaos theory into motion. Like ripples from a stone in a pond, the effects of those words would touch every aspect of their lives in the months to come.

The next day, Rob went to see Phil, his arch nemesis or, as Rob considered him, more like his arse nemesis, to accept the Munich role.

Phil saw him coming, probably both physically and metaphorically.

"Ah, Herr Robert! What news from the front?"

Assuming that Phil was asking how his discussion with Sue had gone, and that he wasn't suffering from a well-deserved blow to the head, Rob engaged.

"I've had the chat with Sue. Looks like we can make this work. So, yes, it's a goer."

"Awesome sauce, matey. I'll get the paperwork sorted with the finance gremlins and let you have it. All systems go, best warn all the frauleins, eh"? Phil continued, in what seemed, to Rob, to be some sort of reincarnation of Del Trotter with rabies.

Over the next few weeks Rob got everything in order at home and in Munich ready for his impending first three-week stint in the new office. To be honest, the thought of going filled him with apprehension, it was going to be a long slog and he wasn't a fan of working away from home at the best of times since he'd met Sue.

But, as November arrived, it was time for Rob to depart.

Sue drove him to the airport, there was little discussion in the car about Munich, just planning how to deal with things on the home front whilst he was away and then at home again. Rob was struck by how well Sue handled these sorts of things, no fuss, just straight into managing the job at hand. He wasn't even entirely sure anybody would notice he was missing for three weeks, which was strangely reassuring, in a way.

With a swift peck and loving hug, he said his farewell to Sue in the airport car park and dragged his battered suitcase up the pathway to the Departures terminal and readied himself to do battle with the usual airport security queues.

As he checked his suitcase in, Rob pondered the imponderable of what lay beyond the little rubber curtain, what adventure did the baggage go on once it was on the other side? Was it some elaborate Wonka-esque system of tubes and conveyors, or just some sweaty guys with tattoos heaving them onto a trolley?

Once he was airside, Rob planted himself in a coffee shop and waited for his boarding call.

Even the flight wasn't something he was particularly looking forward to, booked into the cheapest cattle class seats, as usual, with nothing but an overpriced plastic sandwich to look forward to.

Eventually, the call for the 13.50 flight to Munich was tannoyed and he headed for his departure gate.

Chapter Two - Bavaria

Rob's flight arrived at Munich in the late afternoon, and he was soon reunited with his suitcase, thankfully fully intact given the length of his stay.

As he headed from the gleaming, elaborately arched, glass roofed terminal to the taxi rank outside, the enormity of his decision hit him. He was here for weeks, or even months, and he didn't even know enough German to get a taxi to his hotel without looking a complete clown!

He delved deep in his memory banks, way back to the lone school year when he'd tried taking German as an option. That was all he had; it wasn't much but it was going to have to be enough until he picked up a bit more. It would be a struggle though; he wasn't sure that being able to ask for a beach ball to be taken to the station was likely to be of any use.

He needed some help from internet translation sites on his phone, thank God for Google he thought.

Somehow, he successfully managed to get a taxi from the airport to his hotel in the city centre, more due to the taxi driver's English than Rob's German. To Rob's delight, the hotel receptionist spoke near perfect English and all the arrangements had been made correctly, so another hurdle had been cleared (more than once Rob had arrived at hotels on business to discover problems with his booking, major problems).

Rob retired to his hotel room to unwind for a while and unpack. Once in the immaculately clean and crisply arranged room, he kicked off his shoes and set about disgorging the contents of his battered suitcase. For a change, it was actually worth emptying the suitcase, he was here for three weeks but was more used to living from the suitcase one night at a time on previous business trips.

He delved into the dark recesses of the suitcase and produced a toiletry bag, adorned with slightly faded pictures of some non-descript children's television characters. He hadn't been too bothered about what he'd packed his stuff in at home but now was starting to feel a little sheepish about three weeks of hotel housekeeping staff admiring his age-inappropriate toiletry bag in the bathroom.

With that Rob, gave an inner shrug and walked to the bathroom with his toddler's toiletry bag. As he clicked the chrome light switch, the fluorescent lighting came on with a familiar clunk, clunk, burr sound. The lighting seemed very white and clinical against the gleaming white tiles of the bathroom. As hotel bathrooms went, thought Rob, this was delightfully clean compared to some he'd stayed in that looked like they'd been recently used for tractor repairs.

Returning to the bedroom, he flung himself onto the bed and started to scour the television channels for anything that he could actually understand, eventually settled on a 24-hour news channel which was, at least, in English.

After a pleasant, if somewhat sad and lonely, dinner for one in the hotel restaurant and the obligatory phone call home it was time for Rob to get some sleep ahead of his first day in the new office.

The new day dawned, and Rob was up at 6am, ready for breakfast and an early start at the office.

The day's first obstacle would be finding the office! Rob checked the street map on his phone, in an unexpected piece of good planning, his company had, for once, booked a hotel within reasonable walking distance of the office so things were looking good, so far.

Rob strode out of the hotel reception, down the marbled steps and into the crisp Bavarian morning, laptop bag in hand and headed confidently for the office.

Ten minutes later, Rob strode less confidently past the hotel steps having realised he'd gone in the wrong direction. At least those ten minutes had given him an opportunity to savour a little of Munich's charm and, frankly, cleanliness compared to a similar stroll near his office in Bristol.

Rob found Munich to be, from his first impressions, rather grander than he'd really expected. He'd not really accounted for its importance in Bavaria, or indeed Bavaria's importance in Germany as a whole. The town seemed to be a combination of relatively grand older buildings, punctuated by gleaming glass fronted modern office buildings. To Rob, it didn't seem too dissimilar to Bristol, just a little cleaner, a little crisper, a little more…. well, German.

On the whole, he was beginning to feel like, just maybe, this job wasn't going to be the huge mistake that he'd feared it might be. Perhaps, for once against the run of form, this job wasn't going to suffer from Phil's reverse Midas touch as so many others had.

Buoyed with this newfound sense of optimism, Rob finally arrived at the Environmental Group office building and presented himself at reception for the obligatory identity checks and building induction presentation. All rather dull but a necessary evil on the first day in the new office, besides it killed a couple of hours as an alternative to actual work.

At 11am, photos taken, pass issued and his induction complete, Rob was told to wait in reception and that someone from his floor would fetch him shortly to show him to his desk.

A few minutes later, a smartly dressed woman in her forties appeared at the reception desk and promptly headed in Rob's direction, her smart shoes clip clopping across the polished floor as she approached.

"Robert"? She asked with a friendly smile spreading across her face.

Rob nodded, "just Rob" he replied.

"I'm Maxine, I'm the office manager for your department. Please, come with me."

With that Maxine strode off in the direction in which she had come from with Rob a pace behind.

As the pair headed towards the lifts, Maxine made Rob start to feel much more like he was going to get on OK in this role. She was enthusiastic about her new role and keen to talk about anything and everything with her new colleagues.

Rob felt like he already had a new friend, and that would be a priceless asset as he settled into life in a new country.

Maxine showed Rob to his desk and, much to his personal delight, the kitchen area where there was coffee…. real coffee, not some steaming brown ooze pretending to be the real stuff. Small victories, these all mounted up in Rob's mind.

Over the next couple of days, the rest of the office team arrived from various organisations across Europe and took up their new roles. Most were in small teams who'd worked together elsewhere so Rob was starting to feel a little on the periphery of things from a social perspective and he gravitated more towards his new friend, Maxine.

Life in the office was polite and professional, that was a little unexciting to Rob but certainly made a pleasant change from occasional visits from Phil in the guise of some sort of environmentally focused mobile meat stall vendor.

Rob was gradually spiraling his way out further afield from the office in search of lunch each day, as he'd suspected it wasn't all "lager and bratwurst" has Phil had seemed convinced. Aside from the occasional feeling of being "Billy

No Mates" in the office, Rob was actually starting to get quite used to being in Munich.

On Friday, Maxine announced to the assembled team that she had arranged a low-key welcome party for them at her apartment on Saturday night. The thought of this didn't exactly fill Rob with joy, Saturday night talking shop with a bunch of middle-aged men of different nationalities wasn't high on his bucket list, even in a new town.

He thought, just maybe, he should make his excuses to Maxine and dodge that particular fun deficient bullet.

"So, Maxine, about the party tomorrow……" he hesitated.

"You're trying to not come along"? She probed, he was busted, she'd seen through him already.

"Well, err, yes. I don't really know anyone that well and, to be honest, I'll just end up being a grump in the corner all night."

"Well," she said, "you won't be the only lonely grump there. My friend Vanessa is coming along, and she doesn't know anyone at all there."

"Why's she coming along then"? He asked with total bemusement, after all why would someone volunteer to attend the party equivalent of watching paint dry if they didn't have to?

"Her husband left her. She's hardly been anywhere for the last few months, that's not good for a girl like Vanessa. You can compare grumps."

So, firmly placed in his box, Rob resigned himself to a Saturday night of work talk and whatever the German equivalent of pineapple and cheese on sticks was. If there was any sort of test available, Rob was quite sure this party would come out entertainment negative.

One week down, two more to go before I go home for a week, was all Rob could think about that night as he lay, alone, in his hotel room. Home again, to Sue and the kids, back to his old familiar, his one safe place.

Chapter Three - Chaos finds a name

Saturday came and Rob decided to take a longer walk around the centre of Munich during the day to see a few sights and, hopefully, stock up on a few small talk topics for that night's party. That much, he had to do, he was resigned to turning up and toughing it out as long as he could, or at least as long as seemed polite before escaping into the night.

By 7pm, there was nothing else to be done apart from heading across town to Maxine's apartment for the party. To avoid the airport taxi clown issues, Rob had booked a taxi online and the journey there was hassle free, another small victory to chalk up.

Rob pushed the button marked "Kohler" and moments later Maxine buzzed him in on the intercom. After two flights of stairs, he was soon in the apartment with an assortment of office colleagues and a jovial middle-aged man he didn't recognise, who turned out to be Maxine's husband and yet another not so willing participant in the festivities.

As he had feared, Rob found soon himself in a discussion on ground water contamination plumes with some Dutch and Belgian colleagues, all very erudite but not in any way, shape or form something that could be construed as enjoyable.

Things were taking the downturn that Rob had expected, this was shaping up to feel like a long night.

And then, although he didn't realise at the time, the moment his life would change forever, as a vision entered the room.

A torrent of perfectly tousled blonde hair, cascading around her face. A face that made him miss a breath as he was drawn to her steel blue eyes, perfectly framed by her smokey eye shadow. Her eyes caught his, and lingered for a second, he instantly felt like he was hooked, her glances pulling at him like a magnet. Rob suddenly felt like a flailing marionette, with no control over his own body, simply dangling by strings from across the room.

Across the room, his gaze was unbreakably fixed on her, he desperately wanted to look away, to act cool but he couldn't. His heart was pounding and yet he felt strangely focused. In his mind the silent queries "why am I staring at her?", "do I look like a psycho, staring like this?", "have I got my mouth open like a guppy fish at feeding time?".

All this happening in his mind overloaded his senses, it made the room seem silent, all the dull hubbub was tuned out, and the room seemed empty, empty, that is, apart from her. For these few fleeting seconds, she was the sun and the moon, nothing else existed.

Still trapped in his trance, he vaguely noticed Maxine talking to the vision, laughing and smiling, shooting an occasional flirtatious glance in his direction. Clearly, she was good friends with Maxine, then it dawned on him that this must be Vanessa.

With that, he was abruptly snapped from his trance by Maxine nudging him.

"Hey" she said, "come back to earth."

"Sorry, I was miles away there" he spluttered, now a little flustered like he'd just woken up.

"I've got someone you need to meet" and with that Maxine grabbed his hand and guided him through the seemingly faceless crowd until there he was, standing before her.

"Rob, this is Vanessa."

Four words that would turn his world inside out, the beginning of all his dreams and nightmares rolled into a single sentence.

He gazed at Vanessa, he had thought that distance may be her friend, that he was deluded at how she looked. But, no, close up she was almost hypnotically attractive, he found himself silently taking in every inch of her face for what seemed to be an age, obviously far too long...

"Wie geht es dir"? She asked.

Panic, sheer blind panic smashed into him, his German was appalling, he had no idea what she had just asked him. He was spiraling down in a ball of flames before he had even uttered a word to her.

"Ich habe sehr kleine Deutsch" he stuttered.

"Sehr kleine"? She asked, a slightly wry smile now developing across her pink glazed lips.

"Ja, von schule, von dreizehn, vierzehn jahre" he murmured, trying to desperately recall his one year of German lessons at school and trying to avoid calling her an umbrella or the like.

"OK, maybe we should just speak English then" Vanessa replied as a radiant smile and slight chuckle appeared, she'd been playing with him, she obviously already knew from Maxine that his German was hopeless.

The sense of relief washed over him, and was clearly not lost on Vanessa, she touched his arm and leaned closer.

"Sorry, I was just joking with you" and another giggle, she was enjoying the moment.

"Well, I'm glad I've already put a smile on your face" said Rob, "you looked about as excited by this party as I am, well was, I'm enjoying it more now."

Vanessa leaned closer again, "you know, this party is really bad, let's go somewhere else and you can see some more of Munich."

What a choice thought Rob, stay here with a bunch of middle-aged guys talking about work or head off into the city with Vanessa? There was no contest.

Without a word from either of them, Vanessa grabbed Rob's hand and they headed for the door. Only stopping briefly to sweep up Vanessa's jacket as they left.

As they stepped out into the cold Munich night, Vanessa slipped on her black leather jacket and Rob finally started to notice things about her apart from her face. She was slim and not as tall as he had first thought, just wearing precariously high heels with her gold dress. Immaculately turned out and stunningly attractive, she wasn't the lonely grump he had been expecting to appear.

Vanessa produced a phone from her jacket pocket and made a short call. Rob didn't really know what she'd said on the phone but a few moments later a taxi appeared for them and headed into the centre of town.

Eventually, the taxi dropped them off and Vanessa guided Rob down a cobbled street to a small bar. It was a quiet, intimate sort of a place, from the clientele it appeared to be trendy but not painfully so.

As they walked in, the lady that Rob assumed to be the owner rushed out to greet Vanessa with a huge hug and a cheek kiss. Clearly, Maxine wasn't the only one who thought Vanessa had been hidden away for too long.

The lady showed Vanessa and Rob to a quiet table near the back and, moments later, reappeared with two foaming glasses of lager for them.

Rob was about to mention that he didn't really drink these days when he decided he should just go with the flow and appreciate the absurdity of this situation…. I'm drinking lager in a bar with a total stranger who, honestly, looks like a super model, this is a crazy town, he thought to himself.

As the evening progressed, their conversation flowed with ease, no doubt assisted by an occasional resupply of the local brew appearing as if by magic.

Vanessa, it became apparent, was no grumpy housewife as Maxine's description had seemed to suggest. Far from it, she was a successful businesswoman with a chain of half a dozen fashion shops across Bavaria. This was one very punchy lady, very much more so than Maxine had ever let on.

The conversation eventually broached the topic of her, soon to be ex, husband.

"My husband was a photographer" she said "well, he still is a photographer, he's just not my husband now"

"So, what happened"? Rob asked with genuine concern, Vanessa was really coming across to him as just needing to talk to someone. He was happy to be that someone with no ulterior motive, no agenda, no strings, he was a happily married man, after all.

"He left me for a 20-year-old model that he'd been shooting."

"That's terrible. The guy is obviously crazy" Rob interjected, again with genuine concern for Vanessa.

"It's better he's not in my life now. I think he just wanted me for money, so it is better that he's gone" she replied.

Rob was starting to see that Vanessa was a far tougher cookie than she let on, there was something innately attractive about that. Not that she needed to be any more attractive, Rob was still mesmerised every time he looked at her.

It was close to midnight when the pair finally left the bar.

Vanessa called a taxi and dropped Rob off at his hotel before carrying on to her home.

As Vanessa's taxi disappeared into the night, Rob was suddenly struck dumb, he was a fool! He hadn't got Vanessa's number! He was an even bigger fool, he had a loving wife at home, what the hell was he thinking?

As he drifted into a slumber that night, he was wracked with guilty feelings that he shouldn't be thinking of Vanessa, but he couldn't stop seeing her face whenever he shut his eyes.

On Sunday, Rob awoke and gave himself a stiff talking to, it was madness to dwell on a woman like Vanessa and, as for taking it any further than he had, cheating had never been his style, ever.

Hopefully, Rob thought, the new working week would bring some welcome distraction from any thoughts of Vanessa and that would be an end to it.

Chapter Four - The visitor

Monday – the new week rolled in, and Rob headed to the office, his new Munich routine starting to feel more familiar and comfortable now. He felt like he was starting to settle in, almost starting to feel at home, almost.

Rob hoped that the new work week would help him move on from Saturday night, to put his Vanessa related madness firmly behind him, sadly he was wrong.

The immediate topic of conversation across the office on Monday morning was the party on Saturday night, but luckily for Rob, the idle chatter revolved around who said what to whom rather than anyone mentioning his abrupt departure with Vanessa. He hoped that their departure had been so abrupt as to not catch anyone's attention, the perfect crime perhaps.

That illusion was comprehensively shattered when Maxine arrived, with a knowing smile etched on her face.

"So, Rob, how did you enjoy the party"? She asked with a tinge of sarcasm in her voice.

"Well, errr…." he stumbled to find a reply, how was he getting out of this conversational bear trap?

"Relax, I'm kidding with you" she said, "I'm glad you and Vanessa went and had a good time. I love her like my sister, she needs to be having good times".

Maxine continued, obviously now getting into her conversational stride.

"He really hurt her, that asshole she married. She needs someone strong. She's a very strong girl but, you know, she needs a rock to hold onto."

There was nothing Maxine had just said that Rob could disagree with, from what he'd seen of her, Vanessa was clearly a very determined woman but with the occasional chink in the armour plating she liked to project to the world. For all the diamond hard exterior, he could see there was a warmth that others seemed to be oblivious to.

Mentally though, Rob was still conflicted, he wasn't the sort of guy who would rush out and have an affair, he knew plenty of those, they were sleazy to a man, not company Rob could see himself in. He loved his wife madly, deeply and would go to the ends of the earth for her. If she asked, he would bring her the moon, no matter the physical cost.

And yet, he was still struggling to shake his thoughts of Vanessa. He had feelings for her, what they were he wasn't sure but there was only one sensible way to sort this out permanently.... not see Vanessa again.

Easy, he thought, she doesn't work here, and I don't have her number, no way to contact her means no contact with her.

So, with his mind made up on the way forward, he threw himself into his work for the day and succeeded in blocking out any further thoughts of Vanessa, at least for a few hours.

Just before 5pm, Maxine took a brief phone call and then strode purposefully over to Rob's desk.

"Are you finishing for the day now"? She asked.

"Yes, that's enough for today" Rob replied with a hint of relief as he stretched in his chair.

"Good. Because you have a visitor in reception. Best to hurry, she doesn't do waiting" Maxine had a twinkle in her eye as she said that it could only mean one thing.

Rob was suddenly enveloped by a wave of emotions. She was here, Vanessa, he couldn't avoid her, he didn't want to avoid her, he had to see her.

He grabbed his coat and walked to the waiting lift. As he pressed the illuminated button for the ground floor he felt his heart racing again, he was excited yet terrified of what all this may lead to.

As he emerged from the lift on the ground floor and looked across the reception area, he was greeted with the unmistakable sight of Vanessa, standing with her back towards him and gazing out of the window. Her blonde hair spilled down across her black leather jacket, a short turquoise skirt protruding below the waist of her jacket and the whole teetering atop some very high heels.

She turned to face him, and at that moment, he felt like he'd been dragged across the room. This was something new, he'd never experienced anything like this before. He had no idea what this was, but he knew it wasn't something he could resist, he knew this could spell disaster for his contented life, but he had to know how this would play out.

That was the moment that he instinctively knew that, if she wanted him to, he would be there for her through hell and high water.

"Hi" that was all she said, it was all she needed to say, no one word would ever have so much impact on Rob's life, or on the lives of his family.

"Hi" he replied, "I'm glad you came."

"I had to; I had a great time with a crazy English idiot who didn't get my number"

She smiled; she knew she was the only thing in his world right now "how were you planning to find me? Some crazy Cinderella thing with a shoe"?

For once, Rob felt relaxed enough to inject some humour into the situation "No, I was just going to ask Maxine for it. And your shoe size"

"Come on, let's eat or do you want me to starve as well as wait for you?"

"Hopefully, you're ordering the food, with my German god knows what we'd get."

"You'll be fine as long as you can say Big Mac in German," Vanessa let out a full-blown laugh, she looked happy, the happiest Rob had seen her, and it was a fabulous sight to behold.

Far from being an empty joke from Vanessa, they did end up in a McDonalds, a rather incongruous setting for Rob to be sharing another great time with someone who, he was beginning to see, was the woman of his wildest dreams and was in serious danger of becoming the centre of his universe. But, once again, the conversation just flowed and the joy of being in each other's company was, by now, plain to see.

After their rather low rent dinner, the pair moved on to the Old Town, where Rob had never ventured before. The spectacle that awaited Rob was incredible to his eyes, stretching out in front of them were the interwoven squares and narrow streets, lined with impressive buildings adorned with towers or crenellations. To Rob, this was how he would have pictured Bavaria if he'd been asked.

This foray into the Old Town was no mean feat on Vanessa's part as cobbled streets don't mix well with high heels. Aside from a few stumbles, which Rob was happy to catch, the pleasant evening passed without incident.

As they prepared to part ways once more, Vanessa grabbed Rob's phone as he took a photo of her.

"There, now you have my number. No need for crazy shoe stuff. Call me tomorrow"

Call me tomorrow…from most women, that demand might seem needy but from Vanessa it was more of a warning…call me or I will know not to waste my time on you.

Rob had no intention of crossing that line with Vanessa, he was going to call her, no doubts entered his mind about that.

Again, she disappeared into the night in a taxi, but this time was different, this time Rob's mental conflict was missing. This time Rob knew he had to see her again and he would see her again, this train was in motion, and he had no idea how things would go, either here or at home.

The one thing he did know was that he would call her tomorrow and tomorrow couldn't come around fast enough.

Chapter Five - Staying in

Tuesday, in most work weeks Tuesday is a non-entity, the day with the worst traffic, an insignificant blur somewhere between the beginning of the week and the end of the week.

But today, Tuesday was special, Tuesday was full of excitement and anticipation for Rob.

Today Rob would be calling Vanessa, he was nervous but bubbling over with anticipation of speaking to her and it showed.

As soon as he set foot in the office, Maxine immediately spotted the spring in his step and pounced.

"Somebody is very happy today. Maybe, they had a hot date last night"?

"Maybe they did" teased Rob, unable to hide his optimism as he headed for his desk.

This cryptic response was like a red rag to a bull for Maxine, something was going on and there was no way she wasn't going to hear about it. She swiftly pulled up a chair at Rob's desk and proceeded with a friendly but firm interrogation. After all, this involved her dearest friend.

"So, how did you get on with your surprise visitor yesterday"?

"It was great. Haven't you spoken to her yet"? Said Rob, genuinely surprised that the two wouldn't already have discussed every detail.

"She couldn't talk earlier, having a spa day, sounds like she has big plans tonight."

"Oh" said Rob, trying to retain a façade of calm, but inside he was thinking shit, shit, shit! I won't be able to speak to her, even if I do, I won't be able to see her tonight.

He was deflated, suddenly the spring had gone from his step, excitement was now replaced by a strange, empty feeling. Rob trudged, uninterested, through his work until it got to around 2pm when he thought he should call Vanessa now anyway, even if she didn't answer at least, he had made the call.

He looked in his phone contacts and found a number simply named "V", he called the number and waited, anxiously.

It rang three times and then a familiar voice came through the earpiece.

"Hallo."

"Hi" said Rob, his spirits now starting to take an upward turn at last.

"You called me then."

"Yes, you told me to, so I did. Did you think I wouldn't"?

"Not really, but you kept me waiting. You know I don't do waiting" a light giggle crept through with the final words. That was an enormous relief for Rob, now he knew she was just toying with him again.

"Maxine says you have plans tonight, should I see you tomorrow instead"?

"Yes, I'm having drinks tonight, but you're included, if you'd like to."

"Of course, I'd like to" he said without hesitation and with possibly the biggest understatement of his life, if she'd said she was unblocking the drains tonight he'd still have been there.

"OK, 6pm here, I'll message you my address so you can book a taxi" and with that she was gone.

Sure enough, a few minutes later Rob's phone pinged and lit up as a message came in from "V"

Wasting no time, he booked his taxi and made plans to leave work early so he could change his clothes and eat quickly before going to meet her.

That evening, his taxi arrived at Vanessa's address without issue, although the journey had taken quite some time, Rob had no idea if this was because the taxi driver had taken him the long way or if he was on the outskirts of the city.

Rob checked his watch, 5.55pm, he couldn't turn up 5 minutes early and catch her unprepared, that would not be popular. So, at the risk of looking shifty, he decided to wait at the bottom of the drive for a few minutes.

That gave him time to take in his surroundings, he had no idea where he was, but he was obviously in a well to do area of town judging by the manicured gardens and multiple BMW and Mercedes parked on the driveways around him. On this driveway sat a gleaming black X3, presumably belonging to the lady of the house.

The night air here was quiet, not quite silent but missing the background burble of the centre of the city.

He checked his watch again, 6.01pm, time to go to the door.

He knocked the large, chrome knocker on the door twice, emitting a solid, heavy thud with each blow.

The door opened to reveal Vanessa in a short black dress, with a broad diamanté choker that twinkled under the spotlights in the hallway, her hair and makeup were perfection, as ever.

"6.01, you're late" she joked, this time with not even a pretense of annoyance.

"Sorry, I was spotting cars in your street" he quickly replied with a smile.

Rob walked into the house as she shut the door, white marble tiled floors stretched in every direction, with minimalist black and chrome furnishings in each room that he could see. Her heels clacked resoundingly as she walked on the tiled floors behind him.

"Wow, amazing" he blurted out like a reflex reaction as he looked around him.

"Me or the house"? She asked.

He turned towards her, she looked incredible, even more so than he had seen her look before, if that was even possible. The spotlights once again catching the diamantes on her choker, sending sparkling shafts of light through her long, blonde hair. Her eyes shimmered blue in the harsh white light of spotlights, making them impossible to escape from being drawn into.

"The…the house is amazing" he stuttered.

"Oh, so not me."

"No…you are beyond amazing…. I…I have no words for how incredible you are."

Quickly changing the subject before he started to sound any more sickeningly fawning than he already had, Rob asked "so what is the plan tonight"? He was assuming that there was a destination or guest list involved, that he would need to be prepared and on his best behaviour.

"Well, my plan is to go in there and drink that wine" she said pointing to the softly illuminated lounge where a bottle of red wine sat, uncorked, on the low table with two glasses.

This caught Rob entirely by surprise, he had not seen this coming for even a moment, he was off guard, disorientated. This seemed to be a frequent occurrence where Vanessa was concerned, she could disarm him at any given moment, with consummate ease.

Vanessa walked into the lounge and poured a little wine into each glass, holding one out in Rob's direction. He walked towards her and took the glass from her hand.

She took the other glass and, still standing in front of him, raised it saying "we should have a toast to my good friend, Maxine. I have a lot to thank her for in my life."

With that she took a sip from her wine, but Rob didn't, he was too enthralled just watching her, her hair, her eyes, her lips. Once again, he was being pulled into her blue eyes and nothing else existed in the room, in the world even.

Standing there, transfixed by her gaze, he didn't notice her place the glass on the table. He didn't notice anything until her lips grazed against his. That caught his attention, as she stroked his cheek with her perfectly manicured hand. Her gaze though was gone, her eyes were closed as she kissed him, he wanted to hold her, but he just stood there, paralysed.

She pulled away slowly.

"Is that not OK? I'm sorry, I just thought…." she said, decidedly concerned that she'd overstepped the mark.

"Oh my god… that is so OK…please don't ever stop" he jumped in quickly, there was no way he wanted her to think he wasn't interested.

They kissed again, this time he held her waist like his life depended on it, letting her go just wasn't an option anymore.

"I want you to stay with me" she whispered to him.

He loosened his grasp on her waist and she took his hand, leading him to the bedroom.

The next morning, Rob woke to find Vanessa asleep, spooned against him, his face delightfully buried in her long blonde hair. All he could see now was Vanessa, all he could smell now was Vanessa, all he could hear now was Vanessa's gentle breathing as she slept alongside him. His world contained only Vanessa now, this was not the first time he'd had that feeling with her but this time the reality matched the feeling.

His life seemed better now that he had her in it, there was no way to know where this would go but he had to find out, this was a voyage that he had to be on until journey's end, wherever that may be.

Chapter Six – Home?

Over the next few days, Rob saw Vanessa every day. He couldn't think of anything else each day, he found he was just eking out an existence between opportunities to see her.

Things were going well between them, perhaps a little too well, as the elephant in the room began to drift into view…at the end of his third week, Rob would be returning to England for a week.

This had started to cast a long shadow on Rob, much as he craved his time with Vanessa, he was now fretful about his impossible new conundrum - how could he leave the woman he loved, to return home to the woman he loved?

This ate away at Rob; Vanessa could see that he was troubled and had guessed the cause. To add to the conundrum, she wasn't happy being the other woman and inflicting on Rob's wife the same hurt that she had been through. But, like Rob, she was unable to step away, she was unable to step off the moving train.

Rob was rapidly reaching a state of turmoil, his wife couldn't find out about Vanessa, but he couldn't possibly ignore Vanessa for a week. Even his thoughts of only making stealthy daytime calls to Vanessa so his wife wouldn't find any incriminating texts or missed calls seemed, somehow, like he was caging Vanessa. This wasn't the way he should treat her; he couldn't treat Vanessa like that.

Eventually, the third Friday was upon them, the day Rob had looked forward to all those weeks ago, was a day that he now dreaded. How could "home" still feel like his home when all he wanted to do was be away from it, to be far away from it, with Vanessa?

Rob made his way to the airport, alone, lost in his thoughts. Vanessa had decided to avoid any tearful farewell at the airport, "I don't do my crying in public" was the phrase still bouncing around in Rob's head as he walked into the Departure building.

Rob walked reluctantly to the check in desk, struck by the one constant in his life, with all the upheaval of the last three weeks the only thing unchanged since his arrival was the battered suitcase trundling behind him.

Rob watched his trusty case vanish through the rubber curtain of the baggage conveyor and then made his way into the terminal.

In a mirror image of his last flight, Rob settled himself down in a coffee shop, once again his mind full of worrisome thoughts and fears, but for all too different reasons.

As he sat, pondering his existence, there was a chime from his phone as a message arrived.

His phone screen popped up a small box, "message received from V."

Suddenly, Rob was back in the room, he needed to see what this message said, his mind raced with all the negatives that it could possibly be, was she coming to her senses and calling it a day? That would be heartbreaking for Rob but would certainly make for a simpler life.

He opened the message, which seemed to take an age to appear, the message simply read "X."

She wasn't calling it a day; he wasn't escaping his predicament that easily.

His flight was called, and Rob rushed to the gate, still in a mental blur about how the hell he could manage the situation he'd brought about.

On the flight, he convinced himself that it would be fine, that once he was at home, he'd be able to put Vanessa out of his mind. Maybe, he thought to himself, I'll come to my senses this week and that will be the end of the whole

Vanessa situation. Out of sight, out of mind, he thought.

Satisfied that he could successfully navigate his way out of this mess, he nodded off until he heard the pilot announce preparations for landing.

As the tyres hit the tarmac with a screech and a jolt, Rob felt like he was now back in the real world rather than this strange parallel dimension that he seemed to exist in Munich.

As he left the terminal with his case in tow everything seemed familiar, but a little dull, as if someone had turned down the contrast on the world.

Sue was waiting for him outside; he was so glad to see her. They hugged, he instantly felt safe with her, he felt at home but….it wasn't there, the almost electric feeling of excitement he felt every time he'd embraced Vanessa, it wasn't there with Sue.

That was a problem, a vast, yawning chasm of a problem that Rob hadn't even begun to think about in his master plan to forget about Vanessa.

The drive home from the airport was filled with discussion of who had done what while he was away and all the mundane details and minutia that people take for granted in their everyday lives.

When it came to questions about Munich, all he could really say was "it was OK, people are nice", this reticence was for the best, suddenly announcing that you may have met the love of your life and she spells impending doom for your marriage is obviously not a good course of action.

The week at home seemed to grind on for Rob, he was there but not really there, his body may have been in that house each day with Sue, but his mind was wandering marble tiled rooms in Munich in search of Vanessa.

He called Vanessa whenever he could, but the skulking and deceit were already taking a toll on him, this wasn't his style. He couldn't keep this up for long and the thought of lying to his wife, on and on, filled him with disgust. Self-loathing was now starting show itself amongst Rob's feelings of guilt and confusion. He was going to have to make a decision, and soon, for the sake of everyone.

Soon enough, the week at "home" was over and farewells were made once more in the airport car park.

Again, he dragged his constant companion, the battered suitcase, into the departure building and bid it bon voyage through the rubber curtain.

He made his way to the same coffee shop and settled down to await his boarding call. He felt, somehow, free now with no need to cover up his feelings for Vanessa. He reached for his phone and sent a message to "V", simply "on my way. X"

Just being able to send that message in plain sight of people was liberating for Rob, this was how he thought he should be able to be, not skulking, not deceiving, not being someone who disgusted him.

With that, his phone pinged, a message from "V" …

"See you at airport. X"

This was a development he had not expected, she was coming to meet him, he was excited and nervous once again, just as he had been when she appeared at the office. This would be them out in the open, feelings on display for all to see. This, he thought, is how it should be.

On this flight, there was no sleeping for Rob, he was agitated, excited at seeing Vanessa again.

He willed the plane to go faster, there was no time to lose in getting him back to her.

At Munich, he snatched his case from the carousel and strode towards the exit doors like a man possessed. The automatic doors opened and there she was, amongst a small crowd of assorted taxi drivers and relatives of other passengers, unmistakable even in a crowd.

He pushed through the crowd and straight to her.

"God, I've missed you" he exclaimed before holding her tight to him.

"Good" she said, "otherwise I would have waited here for nothing, you know how I feel about waiting."

Rob got the distinct impression that, perhaps, that was only partially a joke. It was clear that Vanessa was far from happy with him being away and the subterfuge required to keep in touch was not something she wanted any part of.

Rob felt that his hand was now, very much, being forced into making some hard decisions.

Whichever route he took would cause heartbreak to someone and both would cause the same to him. This, he knew, would be a game

with no real winners, everyone would lose
someone dear to them.

Chapter Seven - Decision Day

Rob awoke on Monday morning, with Vanessa nestled against him. He was struck by the bizarre situation he was in; he had a hotel room in Munich he didn't use now and a house in England that he didn't want to go to, the only place he wanted to be was right here, with Vanessa.

He quietly booked a taxi on his phone and got dressed, taking care not to wake the gently breathing Vanessa, he was a little early for work, but he could use the thinking time in an empty office. As he saw the taxi arrive in the street from the window, he quietly shut the front door behind him and walked down to meet the taxi.

By his reckoning, he had three weeks to make his decision and work out how to deliver that decision to whoever it would affect. Three weeks until he was due to return to England again, maybe it would be the last time he went there, or maybe this would be his last time in Munich, maybe that was his exit strategy for the Vanessa situation….to run away, never to return.

Later that day, his phone pinged with a message from "V"

"We should talk later. X"

This was not good, Vanessa needed to be heard, to Rob this looked like his three weeks of pondering time had now come down to a right here, right now situation. His suspicions had obviously been correct, Vanessa was in no mood to play the secret, other woman any further, she was far too powerful a character to play that role. He had to respect her for that, he didn't enjoy the subterfuge either, but he was too weak a man, too shallow a man to break free from it. She, though, would not entertain it for a moment longer, she was strong.

Rob finished work at 5pm and got a taxi to Vanessa's house. For the first time ever, he was apprehensive about seeing her. This was one of the conversations he knew was needed, but he still didn't know which way he would jump when it came to it.

What he did know was that, with Vanessa, there could be no half measures, no prisoners would be taken - he would either be in or out of her life. She wouldn't tolerate being second fiddle to anyone, she was not to be hidden away in the shadows. Vanessa didn't have that diamond hard exterior for no reason, it was her defence, she had been hurt and would be hurt no more.

He opened the heavy front door and walked in, shouting "honey, I'm home" tempted him but seemed inappropriate given the current situation.

He walked in further and found Vanessa in the kitchen.

"Hi, I let myself in."

"Oh, hi, I'm just making coffee. You want some"?

"Yes, please" Rob responded, not really wanting a coffee but feeling he needed something to occupy his hands as he was feeling so nervous now.

Vanessa walked to the kitchen table and placed the two coffee cups down; she pulled out a chair and sat down.

By now, Rob could feel sweat starting to ooze from his palms and his heart was starting to pound, he was unprepared for this conversation with no idea how he would deal with it.

"So, we have to talk about some things" she started.

Rob pulled out the opposite chair and sat down, he felt rather like a naughty schoolboy being taken to task by his school teacher. Vanessa's tone was calm, measured and yet forceful enough to make her point abundantly clear.

"I can't do this" she continued "I can't be your dirty secret, I'm worth more than that, Rob."

Rob was still searching for words, any words, he didn't even know what he wanted to say let alone how to say it.

Vanessa came at him again "just tell me what it is you want to do, Rob. Let me know where I stand."

"Do you live there, with her, or here with me"?

Rob finally found his voice and, without even really knowing that he'd said it, announced "I'm here, I'm with you…always."

It was done, it was said, the blood seemed to rush from Rob's head, he felt a little feint.

Then the enormity of his decision began to sink in, now he had the even more terrifying task of breaking the news to the unsuspecting Sue and his family. He was turning his back on them and everything they had worked for.

Vanessa broke the silence "You need to think how you tell your wife. You have to tell her face to face; this can't be a phone call."

She was right, this was a horrible thing to be doing and it needed to be done in person, breaking the news by phone would be a new low.

So, the scene was set, Rob's three-week pondering window was now only to consider how to break the news to Sue and the kids. Only…as if it was a mundane, everyday task to destroy twenty years of marriage, to alienate your own flesh and blood.

In his second week, Vanessa announced to Rob that she had to attend a business-related function that evening, and it wouldn't be appropriate for him to attend.

That night, Rob was home alone in Vanessa's house, awaiting her return like an overanxious parent waiting up for a teenage child to return late at night. He knew how that went; he'd done that on a few occasions with Julia already.

Rob waited impatiently, peering from the window at each sound of a car in the street, each time it was a false alarm.

He trusted Vanessa, he didn't for one second believe that she would look at another man, but he was anxious to be with her again, her absence threw a spotlight on his insecurity.

Just before midnight, there was the sound of a taxi outside followed by high heeled footsteps on the driveway and a strange rattling, rummaging noise at the front door. Concerned at what the noise might be, Rob opened the door.

Rob was nearly flattened by a clearly, very drunk Vanessa tumbling through the open door with keys and handbag in hand.

As Rob struggled to maintain his balance as the giggling and staggering Vanessa draped herself around him, he managed to reverse back into the hallway and shut the front door.

Vanessa, now half draped on Rob and half braced against the hallway wall, kicked off her shoes in different directions and kissed Rob, breathing the unmistakable spirit aroma of schnapps over him.

Vanessa was so drunk that Rob decided his only course of action was to put her straight to bed without delay. Half walking, half dragging the near deadweight of Vanessa down the hallway, Rob headed for her bedroom. All along the way, Vanessa burbled drunkenly at Rob in German, he had no idea what she was saying but that was often the case with drunks in England so was hardly new news.

When they arrived at her bedroom, Rob laid Vanessa down on the bed but realised he couldn't just leave her there fully clothed in a designer dress in this state, he couldn't recall Gucci ever being renowned for ease of vomit removal.

He needed to help her out of her dress, normally not a task that he would be daunted by, quite the opposite. But on this occasion, he feared it may be rather like trying to wrestle an octopus into a string bag.

Eventually, he had managed to slide Vanessa out of her dress and had remained vomit free. But now, he thought leaving her in only her underwear would be too cold, he should put her in something warm yet expendable. The only thing to hand was his own t-shirt, so playing out the whole scene in reverse, Rob grappled Vanessa's drunkenly flailing arms and head into the rather oversize t-shirt.

Job done. He rolled the near comatose Vanessa onto her side in the recovery position and slipped the bed linen over her. Using his experience of managing drunken teenage children, he disappeared to the kitchen returning with a large glass of water and a large plastic bowl, now the job was done.

Vanessa, by now, was snoring loudly and dribbling onto her pillow. Combined with the distillery smells and likelihood of vomit, Rob decided that sleeping on the sofa may be wise tonight.

Rob grabbed a spare blanket and headed back to the lounge, settling down on the sofa he dozed off, with a background lullaby of drunken snoring and occasional mutterings in German coming from the bedroom. It wasn't the most attractive he'd ever seen Vanessa but at least he knew she was alive in there.

Around 5am Rob was awoken by the feeling of being tugged by his left arm. Rolling over and opening his eyes a little, he discovered a still rather drunk Vanessa had come in search of him and was intent on dragging him to the bedroom.

Rob duly complied, not entirely sure if Vanessa was even awake or sleep walking and slipped into bed beside her. She nestled against him and was immediately asleep and snoring again.

Rob lay there, unable to sleep, admiring Vanessa in the dim light of the bedroom. It amused him that even in this state, even with the farmyard noises and alcohol smell, she was still fascinating to him.

When it was time for Rob to get ready for work, he quietly dressed and waited for his taxi.

The snoring was a little quieter now and the vomit bowl was still empty, Rob now added some paracetamol tablets to the bedside table beside the glass of water, they'd be needed later.

As he quietly shut the front door behind him, he could still hear Vanessa's snoring drifting through the house.

At around 11am, Rob thought it was time to check in on Vanessa, he sent a message to "V" on his phone "are you alive? X"

A few minutes later, he got a reply.

"I think so" shortly followed by another "thanks for the water. X"

That evening, Rob returned home to a still rather delicate Vanessa.

"So, a bit drunk last night, weren't you?"

"Sorry, was I very bad?"

"Well, you were drunk enough to forget I don't speak German."

"Oh, I'm so sorry. The business chamber had a meeting….and schnapps tasting."

"Ah, that would explain it. How much did you have?"

"Too much. A lot too much"

This episode took on an importance beyond its first impressions; to Rob it proved Vanessa was human, fallible. To Vanessa, it proved that Rob was there for her, he could be trusted, he could be loved.

The following days passed with Rob being a virtual lodger at Vanessa's house, never venturing near his hotel but he kept the booking to avoid any questions from his business.

He was happy to be with Vanessa but still being eaten away by his upcoming trip back to England.

Chapter Eight - Breaking the news

Rob had made his decision, but that was the "easy" part, delivering the news of that decision would be horrific for all concerned.

With Vanessa, the discussion had at least been about the known, with Sue it would be out of the blue. He would be dropping a Vanessa shaped bomb onto on unsuspecting audience.

In a vain attempt at doing the "right" thing, Rob decided he would break the news to Sue on his first day in England and be prepared to make a hasty exit if needs be.

As he left Vanessa at the airport, she only said "I'm sorry. I'll be here when you come back", she knew what Sue was about to experience as she'd been there herself so recently. There was no way Vanessa could take any delight in inflicting this hurt on another woman, even one she'd never met but she and Rob needed to be together, without lies and subterfuge.

Rob arrived back in England to his customary warm but somewhat empty embrace from Sue and said little in the car on the journey home.

Throughout the afternoon, and over dinner, Rob went through the motions of playing at happy families, but he knew he was hiding something from them that would unleash things that he'd thought unimaginable only weeks before.

As they cleared up after dinner, Sue eventually let on that she knew something wasn't right.

"You're very quiet today. What's up"?

Rob briefly considered playing the "I'm just tired" card but thought better of it and braced himself.

"We need to talk."

"OK, about what? Sounds ominous."

Rob reached for his phone and opened the photo of Vanessa he had taken that night in Munich. He placed the phone on the worktop in front of Sue.

"About her."

"Her? Why are you showing me photos of women off the internet. I don't understand"?

"She's not off the internet. Her name's Vanessa and…."

There it was, he had launched the V bomb and all he could do now was wait for the impending barrage of fire and fury that was sure to follow, or so he thought.

Sue looked straight at Rob; he'd underestimated her inner strength at a time like this.

"I think you need to go."

"OK, let me tell the kids I'm going…."

"No. You have to go right now. I'll tell them when the time is right. Just go."

Rob went upstairs to gather his stuff into the battered suitcase and call a taxi.

As he walked back down, he bumped into Kate on the landing.

"Where are you going, Dad"?

"Something has come up, I've got to go back to Munich. I love you sweetheart."

He kissed her head gently and left.

Once at the airport, with no flight booked or hotel, Rob camped out on a squeaky vinyl seat in the terminal building while he tried to book a flight. No flights until the following morning,

Rob had to settle down to an uncomfortable night on the vinyl seats.

By this time, Rob was alone in the terminal apart from a young couple who seemed very much in love. He envied them, their happiness, their togetherness, the boundless optimism of youth. At the same time, he pitied them, pitied that they may end up in the same sorry situation he was now in.

As Rob tried to doze off as best he could, he was periodically awoken by the floor sweeping machine being waltzed past on a seemingly endless route around the building.

He thought of Sue, tearful in their family home. He thought of Vanessa, alone in her house. But here he was, sleeping on a bench with what few belongings he'd swept up into his suitcase. That damned suitcase, it was the one thing in Rob's life with any sort of stable existence, if that thing could talk…. well, he'd at least have someone to talk to right now.

Rob's return to Munich was no triumphant affair, he was sick to his core for what he'd done, and, for her part, Vanessa could understand how Sue must have been feeling.

As the days rolled by, Rob settled into life with Vanessa, gradually becoming more at ease being with her every day. But he was on edge, waiting for the inevitable letter from a divorce lawyer that Sue would have employed….it didn't come, weeks went by with nothing.

Soon, Rob's thoughts turned to something he hadn't given a moment's thought to…. Christmas.

What was he going to do about the kids at Christmas?

There was nothing for it, he was going to have to contact Sue.

He sent a simple message to her number "about Christmas?"

A few minutes later he had her reply, "it's best you don't come, the kids won't want to see you."

This was a real blow to Rob; he'd expected to be an outcast but the reality of it stabbed him through the heart.

Rob decided that all he could do was to send each child a card and a cheque in the post, like a distant relative, which is what he'd become. A brief hand scribbled note to each of them that could never hope to convey any of the things he wanted to say to them.

Chapter Nine - The tourist

By mid-February Rob had still heard nothing from Sue, or any lawyers acting on her behalf, and he just continued paying his share into their joint account as he always had.

But he wanted to reach out, to remind his children that he was still there and still loved them.

After talking his thoughts over with Vanessa, he sent Sue a message "if any of the kids would like a holiday in Munich for easter, we'd love to see them."

He slightly regretted saying "we" but it was the truth, there was no point in pretending that Vanessa didn't exist.

He soon had a curt reply "I'll ask them."

He heard nothing more for a few days and then received another reply "Kate wants to."

This was great news that he'd be able to see Kate but less so that Simon and Julia were clearly not going to be won over any time soon.

Arrangements were made for 15-year-old Kate to fly out alone at the start of her Easter holidays and stay for five days. Enough time to see some of the city and, more nerve wracking, for her to meet Vanessa. Rob had no idea how that would go, they'd all be staying in Vanessa's house together and he didn't understand teenage girls at the best of times.

On the day of her arrival, Rob and Vanessa both went to the airport to collect Kate, much against Rob's protestations about taking things gently, Vanessa had insisted that she should be there too.

As the automatic doors from the Arrivals terminal opened, Kate spotted Rob and rushed straight to him.

"Dad"!!

"Hi, sweetheart. How was your flight?" he asked as he hugged her off her feet, so pleased to see her and even more pleased to see her happy.

"It was OK, a bit boring but you know..."

Kate's eyes then drifted to Rob's left, to the elegantly dressed blonde lady at his side. She looked back at Rob, waiting for a response.

Heart racing now, Rob spoke gently to Kate.

"Kate, this is Vanessa."

Kate took a moment and then blurted out uncontrollably.

"Wow, Dad, she's gorgeous."

This was a surprise all round, even to Kate who clearly hadn't really meant to say that out loud.

Kate quickly took hold of the situation again with youthful exuberance.

"Hi Vanessa. I'm Kate, it's amazing to meet you."

Still reeling from how well that introduction had gone, Rob watched on with disbelief as Kate wandered off arm in arm with Vanessa, chattering frenetically to her newfound friend, leaving Rob to follow on behind carrying her bag.

As the days passed, the trio settled into an unlikely routine of Rob going out to the office leaving the dynamic duo of Kate and Vanessa to get up to whatever it was they got up to. Rob really had no idea what they did each day, whenever he asked either of them, he'd just get the reply "girl stuff" and he'd move on, none the wiser.

There had clearly been shopping trips into the city by the pair and on one occasion he'd returned home to find them both on the sofa watching the television, feet up, with identical dressing gowns and face masks applied.

Whatever "girl stuff" consisted of it obviously agreed with both of them, they were getting along like a house on fire and constantly reducing each other to tears of laughter, usually at Rob's expense.

When the time came for Kate to fly home, her goodbyes at the airport spoke volumes about how things had gone.

"Bye, Dad."

"Bye, Vanessa, see you soon I hope."

All of this was hugely reassuring, even if it did leave Rob a little bewildered as to why it had all gone so well.

With Kate gone again, Rob and Vanessa returned to their routine, making the most of each minute together free from any outside distractions.

This continued until early May when Rob received a message from Sue.

"Julia's 18th, family party 22nd May, 12.30 at the house. Please come."

Rob knew that Julia's 18th was coming up but, given the Christmas situation, hadn't really anticipated attending a party. The fact that he'd been invited was good, an olive branch was being extended and he would be a fool not to accept it.

This did pose one major question to Rob, to take Vanessa or not to take Vanessa?

It was a high risk, his whole family would be there, and he had no idea how he'd be received, let alone how Vanessa would be received.

As he pondered his options, he became more convinced that taking Vanessa was the right thing to do but he needed to discuss it with her first, if she wasn't comfortable with the idea then it wouldn't happen.

Chapter Ten - The unheroic return

As the day of Julia's 18th birthday party dawned, Rob was up early, pacing the floor of the hotel room.

Vanessa stirred, disturbed by the nervous pacing past the foot of the bed.

"Why are you up, why with the stomping around"? came a rather cross query from the bed.

"Can't sleep, busy day."

"What time do we need to be there?"

"12.30"

"What time is it now?"

"7"

"What? Make me a coffee crazy man…and stop with the stomping," Vanessa rolled back onto her side in a vain attempt to get some more sleep.

It was a failed attempt as the clunking and gurgling of the coffee machine reverberated around the room, replacing the rapid pacing that had stirred her.

"OK, OK…. I give up, I'll get up now. That coffee had better be worth it."

She wandered sleepily to the bathroom, muttering in German under her breath. Rob didn't really know what she was saying but was pretty sure it was about him and not complimentary.

The thing that struck Rob at that moment was that, even having just emerged from bed, with no makeup and a case of bed hair…. he still found her absolutely mesmerising, every inch of her profanity muttering self.

Vanessa emerged from the bathroom and made her way back to the bed where Rob had placed a cup of black coffee on the bedside table.

She took a sip and weighed it up, bobbing her head from side to side.

"Not too bad" she said, "you can keep your job."

With that she patted Rob's side of the bed

"Come back. We have plenty of time. Relax."

She was right, Rob climbed back into the bed and shuffled up to Vanessa, resting his head on hers.

Soon it was time for the main event and the preening was underway, Vanessa being at great pains to ensure she made a lasting impression, for all the right reasons. Despite Rob's reassurances that she would look great, even in a sack, she was taking no chances on her first encounter with most of his family.

The short drive from hotel to house seemed over in the blink of an eye and he was pulling onto the driveway for the first time in so long.

He walked up the steps he'd trodden so many times before, in other times, but this time was so very different. This time he was walking up them with Vanessa and his family were assembled inside.

The front door that he'd fitted years before seemed like a foreboding barrier, a boundary between two worlds that would collide the moment he stepped through it.

For the first time in his life, he rang the doorbell of what had been his happy, family home....and waited.

Nothing, no answer, he could hear a burble of voices and activity inside.

He rang the doorbell again.

Still nothing happened on the other side.

Vanessa squeezed his hand, spurred on he drew a breath and opened the door.

As he stepped into the hallway the burble of busy voices from around the house became clearer, and across the background noise he heard the unmistakable voice of his wife...

"Somebody open the door, that'll be your father and his half-dressed German floozy."

With that Sue emerged in the hallway, in a near frenzy of things that needed to be done in time for the big event. Her shocked expression betrayed her inner horror at entering the hallway unprepared, only to be confronted by the sight of a perfectly made up and coiffured Vanessa, resplendent in a powder blue leather trouser suit and obligatory vertiginous heels.

"Hi" said Rob sheepishly.

"You'd better go through" said his wife, gesturing towards the lounge door before withdrawing from the hallway, clearly rattled by the encounter.

As Rob pushed the door open and entered the lounge, he felt a knot of anxiety in his stomach. He stepped into the room and the general chatter ceased in an instant. His entire family were there in the same room, he could feel the unspoken resentment from some about what he had put his wife and family through. But, strangely, from his youngest daughter, Kate, he could also feel warmth, she was genuinely pleased to see him, or rather them.

She had enjoyed her week in Munich and, against all rational expectations, had formed quite a bond with Vanessa. In some ways, maybe that wasn't so odd, for a teenage girl keen on her hair and beauty regime to have this glamorous, blonde goddess parachuted into her life from nowhere must have been a fascinating development.

Feeling Kate's unspoken encouragement, Rob stepped aside from the door and uttered words he'd looked forward to speaking but at the same time had dreaded having to say…

"Everybody, I'd like you to meet Vanessa."

And with that, Vanessa entered the still silent room, looks of fury abounded at Rob's audacity in bringing her here. A few looks of slight bewilderment also flew around the room, was this really the woman that had turned Rob's head so unexpectedly?

Like a knife through the silence in the room, Kate's inappropriately perky voice chirped "Hi

Vanessa, come and sit over here with me" as she beckoned towards the empty space beside her on the brown leather sofa.

Clearly, this was all too much for his eldest daughter, Julia, to bear. She was angry at how her mother had been treated and stormed from the room to find her.

The mood in the room now lightened, a little, as Kate chatted to Vanessa like a friend she hadn't seen in a while. General small talk gradually resumed, and a few polite questions were posed to Vanessa about the journey and how she was finding England compared to Germany.

Now, a little on the conversational sidelines, Rob thought he should go in search of his wife and Julia. There were things that needed to be said, nobody would be looking forward to them and, maybe, it would be best they were said with a smaller audience.

He could make out voices from upstairs, so he nervously edged his way up the stairs, feeling rather like a burglar in what had been, for so many years, his home.

As he walked along the landing, he could make out the conversation between his wife and Julia.

"She shouldn't be here, Mum, he should never have brought her into our house."

"She's here because he's your father and I invited him."

"But not her! Why's he brought her"?

"Because he's with her now and we just have to deal with that, darling."

"Get rid of her, Mum. Tell him to dump her and you'll take him back."

"I can't do that, I couldn't have him back after all this, it's gone too far for that."

"I'm sure he still loves you, Mum, maybe you just need to fight for him … for us."

"Do you honestly think any of us could forgive him for what's happened? What he's done to this family? Besides, you've seen her now, how could I ever hope to compete with her? She's stunning. God, I hate to say this but she's beautiful, I have no idea what she's doing with your father…. maybe she just likes crappy dad jokes."

Rob had heard enough; he quickly entered the bathroom as an excuse for being upstairs.

He stood in the bathroom and collected his thoughts. He stared at himself in the mirror, what had he done? Or, more importantly, why had he done it? The feelings of guilt and confusion started to well up once again, but he took a breath and prepared to enter the downstairs fray again.

Flushing the cistern to avoid suspicion, Rob left the bathroom and walked out, straight into the path of his wife.

"Hi"

"Hi"

"Look, I'm sorry I brought Vanessa without warning you, I'm just…."

"A twat"?

"Well, yes, for so many things, not just that."

"It's fine, really, I had to meet her sooner or later. She seems nice, Kate really likes her."

"She is. No idea what she sees in me."

"I'm just sad that she's not the absolute bitch I'd imagined. I'd love to be able to hate her."

With that, Sue brushed past and went down the stairs to join the throng in the lounge.

Rob followed slightly behind and arrived to hear amused chattering with Vanessa's voice complaining about "stupid, wrong way round cars".

For all the risk in bringing her here, this had worked out OK. With Kate being the only one who had actually met Vanessa before, for the others this had, hopefully, been the revelation that maybe she wasn't the personification of evil that they'd pictured her as.

Chapter Eleven - C

At home in Munich, as he sat peacefully with Vanessa nestled against him, Rob was jolted out of the moment by his phone ringing. He glanced at the screen, "Sue" was displayed across the screen, what did she want? Rob felt there must be a real urgency to this call, Sue hadn't spoken to him unprompted for nearly a year, so why now?

He stood up and answered the phone, Vanessa by now aware from his actions that something was awry.

"Hello" he ventured; it seemed odd to be answering the phone to Sue like this but he couldn't revert to anything more loving as he would have in the past.

"Hi" came the response, Sue's voice seemed hesitant, slightly broken, Rob knew for sure now that something was very wrong.

"Can you talk?" She continued.

"Yes, what's wrong? You sound at the end of your tether."

"I can't really tell you like this… I need you to come home", then the line was dead.

Home…. that one word was like a punch in Rob's face, his home wasn't there now, it was here with Vanessa, but he knew he had to go. Sue would not have asked him to go there without a very good reason, the possibilities seemed endless and terrifying.

Rob could almost feel the colour drain from his face. Vanessa knew instantly what had happened, "You have to go, don't you?" She asked, not really needing an answer.

"Yes. I don't know why, but it's bad whatever it is."

Rob was in a panic as rushed to the bedroom and hurriedly packed his old suitcase once again.

Vanessa booked him onto the first flight out of Munich in the morning and would drive him there herself but there was no question of her accompanying him, whatever this was seemed like something he needed to attend to alone.

The flight and taxi journey from the airport to his former home were consumed with fears of the unknown that awaited him, he was in his own little world of horrifying possibilities.

When he arrived at the house, Sue quietly ushered him straight into the kitchen.

"The kids don't know you're here. I need to speak to them before they know you're here, all the shouting will be a problem otherwise" she said, cryptically.

"What's this about, Sue? There's obviously something really wrong that you couldn't tell me on the phone."

"Cancer…. I've got cancer. The kids don't know yet."

"Christ…. how bad…."

"Bad…Stage 4…it's spread already."

Rob was instantly crushed, this is news you never want to hear from anyone, let alone your wife of so many years. He wanted to hold Sue, to tell her everything would be OK, but he couldn't.

"I'm so sorry, Sue…. I…"

"Look, you didn't give me the bloody cancer, so, for once, this isn't about you."

She continued, with a determination that betrayed how much thought she had put into these words. Sue had obviously known for some time and had been stoically planning how best to tell the family, to make plans for the inevitable and how the children would manage without her.

This was why he had never heard from any divorce lawyers; she had known for some time that this was coming, she had set her mind on keeping things simple at the end, tidy, he was still her husband.

"You need to be back here, for the kids. I'll be able to do less and less, and at some point…. well, you know."

That was that, like it or not, Rob had to return and face the family he had torn apart so recently. This wasn't going to be a week-long trip home; this was going to be long term. With three teenage kids to look after this was permanent, or at least until Kate went off to university in a few years.

Sue called the kids into the lounge while Rob lurked in the kitchen to avoid a scene over his presence. He heard them all go to pieces as Sue broke the news, he desperately wanted to go and console them, but this needed to be her time with them and hers alone.

He stepped out into the garden and found "V" in his phone contacts, he dialed and waited.

"Hi, how is everything"?

"Not good, really not good"

"Why? What is happening"

"It's Sue, she's…. she's dying." Rob could barely hold back tears as he told Vanessa.

"You need to be there for the children. I understand, we'll make this work."

"I'm going to be needed here for years now, you realise that?"

"Yes, I know, I can wait."

"I thought you didn't do waiting?"

"Maybe, this time I try. I see you soon."

Aside from a journey back to Munich to get his gear together, Rob now based himself in the family home once more, or in the spare bedroom to be precise.

The atmosphere was horrific, as Sue became increasingly unwell the children seemed to resent Rob's presence more every day. He couldn't blame them, some of the worst things to happen to any child were being rolled onto them in quick succession. Though he was still, technically, married to Sue and would be there for them, he feared the children emotionally becoming orphans, having lost one parent to cancer and the other to his own stupidity.

As Sue's condition deteriorated further over the coming months, she was eventually moved from the family home to the local hospice, and they were all too aware that meant only one thing.

Sue finally passed on at 2am on a rainy Tuesday morning, with her adoring children by her bed side. Rob was sitting alone in the hallway outside; he had already promised her he'd look after them and couldn't intrude on their final moments together.

In the aftermath, Rob managed to hold things together enough to make Sue's funeral arrangements, the children would make a short eulogy together about their mum but there was no way Rob could, it would seem like crocodile tears to the assembled family. He had so much he would have liked to have said but now he was mute because of what he'd inflicted on his family.

Rob knew that he really needed Vanessa with him at a time like this but there was no way that her presence would ever be accepted at this time.

He would have to deal with this, and the fallout to come, alone.

Chapter Twelve - The Vanessa moment

Now that the post funeral dust had settled, Rob needed to deal with the solo parenting of three heartbroken and understandably resentful teenage children, this was going to be an uphill struggle.

He couldn't ask Vanessa to join him, bringing her into the mix would add petrol to the simmering fire of tension that was present all the time.

He also couldn't go to see Vanessa; he knew he couldn't abandon his children in their hour of need for his own selfish purposes. Vanessa understood this and was as supportive as she could be from afar, but Rob wasn't convinced how long they could make this work.

In Rob's mind, cracks were beginning to show between him and Vanessa, whether real or just imagined, they troubled him, deeply.

But right now, Rob needed to concentrate all his efforts on providing for his children, keeping them safe and secure. A far cry from when he'd walked out on them with such seemingly little concern.

Each day was a battle, with Rob sticking to his mantra of small victories being chalked up each day to keep him sane.

The job of looking after the children was made simpler by their ages so he could take his eye off the ball occasionally but their general antipathy toward him made life tricky every day. Even Kate was, understandably, more withdrawn since her mother's death.

Rob tried his best each day, with Kate he could coax a little conversation each day, with Simon no more than a few syllables and a look of disdain and Julia...well, Julia was the hardest part of the equation. Each day was a tightrope walk, not knowing if she would fly into a raging, shouting attack on him and his behaviour to her mother. That situation was volatile, highly volatile, and the strain took a toll on him each day.

Rob was now in a very dark place; he seldom left the house and had started to look increasingly disheveled. His one solace was occasional music but even that was dark, repeatedly listening to "Heart-Shaped Box", the extreme melancholy of the lyrics perfectly mapping out his own woes. An obsession with those lyrics, the work of a depressed and suicidal mind, were not a healthy sign for Rob. Their dark, insidious undertones sucking any last semblance of hope from him, like a shadowy, melodic leech.

This was now a downward spiral, plummeting from the heights of his times with Vanessa before the cruelest blow to Sue to these new, lonely depths.

As Rob sat alone that night, contemplating the desolate ruins of the life he'd once had, the life he had so unintentionally devastated and the lives of those that had been hurt by the whole saga, he thought about other people, total strangers.

How many people, just like me, he wondered, are there out there who have it all but are secretly yearning for that chance encounter, that crazy attraction, that…that Vanessa moment?

How many of them even begin to understand the devastation that follows in the wake of that Vanessa moment? That everything you love and hold dear will be destroyed before your very eyes? That everyone you love will be hurt and nobody will emerge on the other side unscathed?

Maybe, he thought, there is something about human nature that can't help but want to destroy everything we have that is good, maybe we all secretly hope for a Vanessa moment to bring our world crashing down. After all, people say you feel most alive having faced death, maybe you only truly feel love having faced despair?

How many sad, old gits had he chuckled at with their mid-life crises? What if they were just inescapably driven to pressing a reset button on their life to trigger some futile last rush of adrenaline and cortisol crashing through their bodies? That there was an instinctive drive to feel pain to feel alive, like the underlying temptation to stick your fingers in the whirring blade of a saw? Maybe this was it, maybe his life's work was solely to fuel his own self destruction? Maybe he had spent so long building things up just to have something to tear down?

If he could turn back the clock, surely, he would save things as they were, save his perfect little world, save his children the torment of being caught up in his chaos? But, no, perhaps he wouldn't, because although his life may be contented it would be missing one vital ingredient…. Vanessa.

Chaos had ensued from the moment he met her, but still that fleeting moment when he met her was the first time, he had truly felt alive.

This was his inner turmoil, he couldn't bear that he had destroyed everything he and Sue had strived for but at the same time, he knew he could never live a full life without Vanessa. His eyes had been opened to what could be and, in spite of everything, this had all been worthwhile if he could be with her.

But now, now he wasn't with her, he was a thousand miles from her. He was here, with his children who despised him for loving her, not there with her, she who loved him.

Love…and how was love for him? Was love a many splendored thing? For him, it was a dark and chaotic death spiral that seemed to lead into an abyss.

Rob felt trapped, trapped in this personal hell of his own making. He felt that the very walls of his mind were closing in, crushing him, forcing out any last glimmer of hope.

At that point, the lounge door opened, and Julia appeared, clearly with something to get off her chest. This made Rob more than a little uncomfortable, Julia had been his fiercest critic throughout the whole fiasco, she'd hardly spoken to him since his return aside from rants about "that German bitch", was this about to be another late-night teenage tirade about his treatment of Sue?

"Dad, can we talk?"

"Of course, darling, always"

"I think you need to go."

"What? Go where?"

"Munich...to Vanessa, Dad. You need to see Vanessa."

"But I can't leave you here on your own."

"You can, Dad. And you need to, you're not coping without her, she must be missing you so badly."

"But…"

"Go Dad. We'll be fine, the three of us are old enough now to be here for a few days. Go to Vanessa. You've got this…. we've got this."

With that she hugged her sad wreck of a father and they both sobbed together.

Rob was so happy that Julia had accepted him for who he was, and who he needed in his life. And he knew she was right, the only thing he could draw any comfort from now in this world of despair was Vanessa, he needed her like never before.

Chapter Thirteen - Reunion

In a matter of days from his epiphany with Julia, Rob found himself back in Munich.

Everything seemed so similar to last time he had been here but somehow different, his life had changed dramatically since he'd last been here.

This time there was to be no passionate welcome at the airport, he had told Vanessa he would get a taxi to her house. The public display of affection didn't really seem appropriate now, not so soon after Sue's passing, too much like undertones of a victory parade.

Rob walked up the driveway from the street to Vanessa's door, he banged the knocker twice on the heavy door...and waited.

From inside he heard feint sounds of movement as Vanessa came rushing to the door, flinging it open as she got there.

Rob stood there, he was cleaned up a little from the nadir point of his darkest period, but he was still looking a shadow of his former self, the underlying confidence now gone.

Vanessa took a moment to absorb the sight that lay before her, and then, softly said "I've missed you."

Those few words were what Rob needed, like a shot of adrenaline to his heart, he was instantly back, back in her orbit, where he needed to be.

He stepped in and held her, tightly, he needed to be close to her. As he buried his face in her flowing blonde hair, he wanted to weep, but tears didn't come. They stood for an age, locked in this embrace, neither wanting to break the hold.

Vanessa pulled away slightly, grasping Rob's face with both hands she kissed him lightly and whispered, "I've missed you so much."

They walked to the kitchen where the smell of fresh coffee permeated the air, Rob drew in a deep breath. Since everything that had happened with Sue, he realised he hadn't taken the microseconds to really smell anything and pause to savour the experience, except for the familiar and oh so welcome fragrance of Vanessa as he'd been locked in her embrace.

Rob didn't know where to start, so much had happened since he'd last been with her, but none of it seemed to be the topic of conversation for right now. Right now, all he wanted to do, needed to do, was to drink in Vanessa's radiance, to bathe himself in her love.

There was no need to rush into trying to explain things, he would be here for three days and things would come out for discussion in their own time. The important thing was that he had Vanessa to discuss them with.

Over the course of those three days, Rob gradually managed to articulate everything to Vanessa, and she was a godsend. Far from being the damaged girl needing a rock that she had been when they first met, now she was his rock, this beautiful, steely determined woman was there for him, and he felt safe being with her.

On the day of his departure, they decided that Vanessa would take him to the airport, there would be the public display of affection. There was nothing to hide away from others' eyes anymore, nothing that Rob needed to be ashamed of. She was beautiful, in every sense of the word, and he loved her with every fibre of his being.

As they embraced at the airport, Rob hoped that things would be different this time he left. He knew that, if he needed to, he could be with her, at least for a few days.

With that knowledge, he returned home to his children and set about trying to make some sort of repairs to his relationship with them, a tall order given what he'd put them through.

But at least he had a start, Kate had been a constant source of support throughout and now Julia seemed to have softened to him, a little.

Simon, on the other hand, had shown no signs of wanting to engage with his father. Although, with hindsight, Rob knew that the seeds of that relationship breakdown had been sown long before he had encountered his Vanessa moment.

Simon had, for a long time, been seemingly withdrawn from family life, not wanting to engage with either of his parents, even before Rob walked out of his life. This wasn't anything strange, or even troublesome, he was just a 16-year-old boy doing what teenage boys do. What self-respecting teenage boy wasn't massively embarrassed and annoyed by his parents? Hell, Rob could recall being like that with his own father in his forties!

But none of those things made it easy to establish that relationship afresh, to really unpick what was going on in Simon's world. How could he separate the seething resentment for what he'd done to his family from the seething resentment of every teenager's parents?

He couldn't just start to talk to Simon about his feelings, he'd never talk like that with Rob, he seldom uttered more than a few syllables at the best of times. Rob needed to get Simon out of their usual surroundings, to neutral ground, where they could gradually move onto the subject at hand.

Fishing trip, thought Rob, we used to love fishing when Simon was seven or eight, that's the way to open things up.

Rob knew there was no point in asking Simon if he fancied a fishing trip, he'd get no reply of any use, so he had to just present him with a fait accompli.

At dinner that evening, Rob made his announcement.

"Good news Simon, we're going on a boys adventure on Saturday."

No reply, just a slightly baffled grumpy look.

"Fishing trip, over on the Severn. We've not done that in years, it'll be great."

"Uh, suppose so."

That was the best response Rob could hope for, so things were now in motion,

"You'll be OK for the day, won't you girls"?

Julia and Kate briefly looked at each other as if to ask if the old codger was for real.

"Dad, you're only going 10 miles away, you were in Munich for 3 days and nobody died" chipped in Julia, prompting a snigger from Kate.

"Yes, yes, I forget how grown up you all are now."

By the time Saturday arrived, Rob had made every preparation for the trip, except for knowing how to have the conversation he needed to have with Simon, that would have to be something he did freestyle, and he had to hope the opportunity presented itself.

There was no real conversation during the car journey over towards the Severn, Rob occasionally talked at Simon who never responded, he just gazed unblinkingly out of the window with his ear buds in, listening to something that, from the outside, sounded like a biscuit tin rolling down some stairs.

When the pair had unloaded the car and trudged to their old favourite fishing spot, barely changed over the last eight years or so, Rob set up the tackle and they plopped a pair of small, orange plastic waggler floats into the rippling water.

Rob broke out some cans of fizz and a few fun size chocolate bars in a plastic tub, thrusting the tub in Simon's direction.

The silent teen took a bar and unwrapped it, munching slowly whilst looking out at the water.

As they sat in silence, Rob was calmed by the hypnotic sight of the orange floats dancing on the rippled surface of the water, with the sun sparkling here and there as it hit a passing ripple. He couldn't help but think of Vanessa as the sound of the lapping ripples on the bank gently broke the silence of the scene.

"You know, Si, I'm really sorry about what happened with me and your mum."

No reply, still just staring out at the water.

"It was something I'd never intended to happen. I know you're angry with me, that's only right, but please don't blame Vanessa for any of this. It's not her doing."

This time, Simon's head turned towards Rob but, then away again.

"You broke Mum, dad. You know that"?

"I know. And, God, I wish there was a way I could have avoided that."

"Maybe you could just have left Vanessa alone?"

"I couldn't, I just couldn't. I still can't. I don't expect you to understand, you're still young. You've got a whole life ahead of you. But...but when Vanessa walked into my life, there was no going back for me."

Silence, still staring out at the water.

Rob, himself, felt opened up now, even if he were getting little back in return from Simon, he had to tell Simon what he needed him to know and hope that Simon would be able to give him that opportunity for some small redemption.

"I love her, Si...Vanessa...I love her in a way that I probably never loved your mum, not that I didn't love your mum. God, I did, she was everything to me, but Vanessa was just.... I don't know.... just...."

"Special"? Finally, a response.

"Yeah. I don't know how to put any of this into words. How I feel when I'm with her...."

"You don't need to, Dad. I've seen how you are when you're with Vanessa...And what you're like when you're not with her."

Rob's turn for the silent gaze in Simon's direction, the silent teenager had been taking everything in, processing it in his own way, and now he was ready to speak.

"I don't hate Vanessa, Dad. I don't even hate you for all this. I just miss how things used to be, before you'd ever gone to Munich."

It was all too much for Rob, he broke down, crying uncontrollably into his hands.

As he wept into the darkness of his palms, he felt Simon's hand on his arm.

"I love you, Dad."

After a few seconds, Rob finally regained his composure and stood, looking out at the water. He took a breath and exhaled loudly.

"Come on, let's go home. We never catch any bloody fish here anyway."

Simon chuckled, that was the first time Rob could remember hearing him laugh in so long.

The journey home was a much better affair than the outward-bound journey, consisting mainly of "do you remember that time..." anecdotes from each of them.

Laughter filled the car, apart from when Simon reminded Rob of "do you remember that time when Kate got hit in the face with a swing"?

That one wasn't so funny, Rob had really been hauled over the coals for that, but luckily the egg sized lump on Kate's head faded quickly and Sue's wrath eventually subsided, with only occasional mentions of the incident for the next 12 years.

Chapter Fourteen - A visitor, again

The house was quiet as Rob sat contemplating everything and nothing. The kids had all gone off to school and he had a well-earned day off from work.

There were no particular plans today, no pressing issues to deal with for a change. Today, Rob finally had some head space to process things and recharge himself ready for whatever would come next.

Things at home had taken on a calmer but more mundane routine now. On the plus side, his children didn't seem to hate him quite so vehemently now, but the negative was that he'd had virtually no contact with Vanessa over the last few months.

He was starting to become convinced that she had got tired of waiting endlessly for his troubles to be resolved and had moved on with her life, after all, who could blame her if she had? None of this mess was her doing, she had no need to stick around and deal with any of this.

Rob felt that he was in danger of becoming no more than an annoying, needy friend to Vanessa. She had never given him an inkling that was the case, but he couldn't help worrying that it might be the case.

As a result, his calls and visits to her had become less frequent as he became more convinced that he was just sapping her energy and dragging her down into his mire every time he saw her.

He knew he still loved Vanessa, but he was wary of ruining the life of another woman who loved him.

Around 10am, Rob heard the sound of an engine outside which stopped and then switched off.

Postman thought Rob and headed to the front door ready to intercept today's delivery before it was rammed brutally through the letterbox breaking off the brush strips, as usual.

Rob vaguely made out the shape of a person coming towards the door through the textured glass panels but didn't really focus on any detail before he opened the door.

Expecting to be greeted with the postman's not so chirpy face as the door swung open, Rob almost feinted as he looked out and a wave of emotions rushed over him.

"Hi" came a familiar voice.

There she stood, there was Vanessa, the morning sunlight bringing an other-worldly glow to her blonde hair, half illuminated but half silhouetted by the sun.

He was completely dumbstruck, he had yearned to see her properly for months, but now…no words came to him.

They both stood, silently, for what seemed like an age, he just gazed at her with utter disbelief…. she was here, right now, that was incredible but why was she here?

"Can I come in? I need to pee" not exactly the opening line of any great love story but that was the only conversation that came Rob's way.

"Sorry, come in, come in. I was just so surprised to see you. Oh, toilet is in there" ever the gentleman, Rob gestured towards the cloakroom door.

This was definitely not shaping up into something from Romeo & Juliet, but this was real, unexpectedly real.

Rob walked into the lounge while he waited for Vanessa, he could still picture Vanessa sitting on that sofa with Kate when they had first introduced her to his family.

Moments later, Vanessa appeared in the room, Rob took a moment to fully take in the image before him. She was as beautiful as he'd dared to remember and he'd forgotten how her mere presence seemed to light up a room, or was it to light up his life?

She was holding some car keys out towards him.

"Come, I have to show you something."

"You want me to drive?" asked Rob, slightly confused by what was going on.

"Yes, you know how much I hate the stupid wrong way round cars here."

They made their way out to Vanessa's hire car and got in. Only now did Rob finally find enough words to start to ask what was going on.

"So, when did you get here"?

"Yesterday, I was on the late flight. I stayed in a hotel, ugly place, very dirty."

"Where are we going"?

"This place" she said, handing him a piece of paper with a post code scribbled on it, a very local looking post code.

He typed the post code into the car's sat nav and the destination came up as a village a few miles away.

"Why are we…."

"Surprise" she said, "nice surprise, I hope."

This was intriguing, although he didn't much care where they were going, or why, he was just overwhelmed with relief to be with her again.

After a few miles of hedge lined country roads, the sat nav started counting down in yards and Vanessa told Rob to stop on a roughly graveled lay-by outside a small, neatly kept cottage. It was a stereotypical Cotswold cottage, with buff stone walls and slate roof, between them and the cottage lay a small but delightful little garden tucked away behind a dry-stone wall topped with foliage.

"So, who lives here?" Rob asked, still rather puzzled by how his day was going.

"I do, sometimes now" came the answer he could never have expected.

Once again, lost for words Rob sat silently, mouth slightly agape.

"And when your children leave home, maybe we do" she continued.

Rob opened the car door and walked slowly to the garden gate, he stared towards the cottage, still in disbelief.

He turned back towards the car and found Vanessa was now beside him.

Throwing his arms around her, he held her tightly and never wanted to let go. As he realised that this must be journey's end for them, all his pent-up tears ran down his cheeks and into her golden hair.

Now he was home, now they were both finally home.

The ripples on the waters of Rob's life were finally coming to rest.

About the Author

Guy Charles is new author, based in Gloucestershire in the Southwest of England.

This is his first work of romantic fiction and brings a fresh look at the foolish nature of love and all the chaos that follows in its wake.